Read-Along
STORYBOOK AND CD

What happens when an animal fairy from Pixie Hollow discovers a mysterious creature? To find out, read along with me in your book. You will know it's time to turn the page when you hear this sound. . . . Let's begin!

Printed in the United States of America

First Paperback Edition, February 2015 1 3 5 7 9 10 8 6 4 2

Library of Congress Control Number: 2014940978

V381-8386-5-14353

ISBN 978-1-4847-1075-3

For more Disney Press fun, visit www.disneybooks.com

DISNEP PRESS

Los Angeles • New York

High above Pixie Hollow, a green comet streaked across the night sky. The light was lovely, yet strange. Ancient fairy lore spoke of the very same comet appearing nearly a thousand years before.

The green light spilled into dark corners and
caves, and deep within one . . . something stirred.

The next day the comet was all but forgotten as a tinker-talent fairy named Tinker Bell delivered a large wagon to her friend Fawn. Little did Tink know Fawn wanted to use the wagon to sneak a baby hawk out of Pixie Hollow!

Tink gasped when she saw the hawk. "She doesn't look so babyish to me."

Fawn, an animal fairy, stood firm. "She was when I brought her here!"

Fawn had mended the bird's wing. But now she was well, and it was time for her to leave.

Everything was going smoothly—until Fawn's friend Rosetta offered to help. She sprinkled pixie dust on the berries that concealed the hawk. One by one, they floated into the air.

The hawk screeched and fairies everywhere flew into a panic. Nyx, the leader of the scout fairies, quickly captured the baby bird under a net.

The chaos caught the attention of the fairies' ruler, Queen Clarion. "Is everyone all right?"

Nyx stood tall. "This time. But how am I supposed to keep us safe if Fawn keeps bringing dangerous animals into Pixie Hollow?"

Fawn promised the queen she'd be more responsible and careful.

The following morning, Fawn heard a deep moan coming
from the forest. She followed the sound to the entrance
of a cave. Fawn wanted to see what kind of animal was in
pain, but she remembered her promise to Queen Clarion.
"C'mon, Fawn—listen to your head. Heart gets you in
trouble; head is your friend. No, no, no. Model citizen.
Starting first thing tomorrow!"

Fawn flew into the cave until
she came to an open chamber.
Lying there was the largest—and
strangest—creature she'd ever seen.
"What . . . are you?"

Suddenly, the beast looked at her. Fawn backed away slowly as he got to his feet and unleashed a furious, earth-shattering roar!

Fawn fled the cave as fast as her wings could carry her.

But Fawn was fascinated by the creature. "Isn't it my job as an animal fairy to understand animals? Especially one we've never seen before?"

In the clearing outside of the cave, she watched as the beast stacked up boulders. But he was limping. He had a thorn in his paw. Fawn waited until he was distracted, then pulled it out. The animal was at first startled—then grateful.

Fawn now spent her time observing the creature, but the
only thing he seemed to be interested in was piling up rocks.
To earn his trust, Fawn used pixie dust to place boulders
on the growing mound. The animal grunted his approval.

That night, Fawn slept in the clearing. When she awoke, she found a rock tower looming over her. "Looks like somebody's a night owl!"

Fawn wondered what purpose the tower served. She was full of questions.

Suddenly, the beast grabbed Fawn and put her on top of his head. Then, with a grumble, he stomped into the forest. "Well, you don't have to be so gruff about it. That's it . . . Gruff!"

Gruff stopped in a new clearing and began to build a second tower. Fawn used her pixie dust to float the rocks, and Gruff knocked them into place with his tail. But one time he hit them too hard, and the boulders sailed over a cliff and into Sunflower Meadow!

Fawn knew this would alert the scouts, so she needed to hide Gruff. She shook golden pixie dust in front of him. "Okay, new game, Gruff. It's called 'chase the fairy'!"

But Nyx wasn't far behind. Dodging this way and that, Fawn managed to keep Gruff out of her sight.

Finally, Nyx stopped fast—right at the edge of a cliff. There was no sign of the beast anywhere. "We need to figure out what this is before someone gets hurt."

Fawn knew it was time to show everyone that Gruff wasn't dangerous. She started by introducing him to her friends. "Ladies, say hello to Gruff."

Tinker Bell and the other fairies gasped as Gruff lowered himself from a tree. Fawn explained her plan. "So I'm going to take him to the queen and show her that he's harmless."

Fawn was going to do the responsible thing, just as she'd promised.

But when Fawn arrived, the queen was talking with Nyx. The head scout had found ancient drawings of the comet. The last time it appeared, it had awakened the NeverBeast, a monster that had destroyed Pixie Hollow with lightning!

Fawn said the legend was wrong. She couldn't allow an innocent animal to be harmed. But Nyx was determined to keep all of Pixie Hollow out of danger. The queen asked the two fairies to listen to their hearts and their heads.

It was no longer safe for Gruff in Pixie Hollow. The next morning, Nyx was determined to capture him. The scouts armed themselves and flew after the beast.

Fawn needed to warn Gruff. Knowing he had already built towers in Spring and Summer, Gruff had to be in either Autumn or Winter. Tink headed in one direction, and Fawn went in the other.

Tink found Gruff in the Winter Woods. "The scouts are coming for you!"

Lightning flashed and Gruff swatted Tinker Bell to the ground.

At that moment, Fawn flew in and rushed to Tink's side. But Tink was knocked out. "What did you do?"

As lightning hit the rock tower, Gruff began to grow horns. He ran away from them.

Fawn hurried to get Tink back to Pixie Hollow.

Fawn felt terrible about Tink. She had listened to her heart and not her head, and now one of her best friends was hurt.

Fawn flew back to Gruff and called for him. "Come down. I need to see you."

He seemed happy she was there until the scouts threw a net over him! It was a trap!

Gruff fought, but the scouts quickly covered him with nightshade powder. The beast became drowsy and fell to the ground.

When Fawn went to check on her friend, Tink was awake!
She explained to Fawn that Gruff had actually saved her life.
Lightning had caused a tree to fall. "If he hadn't pushed me
away, I would've been crushed by the tree!"

Determined, Fawn hurried to free Gruff. He was groggy, and his vision was blurred. But he was able to see the glow of Fawn's pixie dust.

Just then, a burst of lightning hit Gruff. His body crackled with electricity. Wings grew out of his back!

Fawn finally understood. "Nyx got it backwards. He's not here to shoot lightning at Pixie Hollow. He's here to draw it away!"

Gruff followed Fawn to the towers. At each one, lightning leapt from the tower to Gruff's horns. There was only one more tower to go!

But Nyx, not understanding its purpose, had knocked the final tower down. Gruff lost his connection with the lightning, and the bolts that had been drawn to his horns scattered everywhere.

A bolt charged toward Nyx. Gruff saved her by taking the blast.

Fawn helped Nyx up. "Don't you get it? He was saving Pixie Hollow!"

Nyx finally understood how wrong she had been.

It was too late to rebuild the final tower. As they looked at the sky, Fawn realized that all the lightning was coming from one spot. She turned to Gruff. "Follow me."

Fawn led Gruff right toward the
vortex of lightning! At the very last
moment, Gruff pushed Fawn out
of harm's way.

In one tremendous flash, Gruff twisted and turned as he absorbed the storm's power. Then he shook off the energy— sending waves of heat and light out over the sea!

The storm was finally over.

Gruff was a hero. In the days that followed, he helped the fairies repair the damage caused by the storm.

The fairies wanted Gruff to stay, but Fawn knew that wasn't possible. "His work is done. It's time for him to go back into hibernation."

Gruff would sleep for 972 years.

The fairies took Gruff back to his cave. They made him a comfortable bed and gave him a fluffy pillow.

Fawn tucked the NeverBeast in and kissed him on the nose. It was time to say good-bye to the best friend she had ever had. "I'm really going to miss you. I love you, Gruff."

With Fawn looking on lovingly, Gruff smiled and drifted off to sleep.